P9-CLC-231

WELCOME TO
PASSPORT TO READING

A beginning reader's ticket to a brand-new world!

Every book in this program is designed to build read-along and read-alone skills, level by level, through engaging and enriching stories. As the reader turns each page, he or she will become more confident with new vocabulary, sight words, and comprehension.

These PASSPORT TO READING levels will help you choose the perfect book for every reader.

READING TOGETHER
Read short words in simple sentence structures together to begin a reader's journey.

READING OUT LOUD
Encourage developing readers to sound out words in more complex stories with simple vocabulary.

READING INDEPENDENTLY
Newly independent readers gain confidence reading more complex sentences with higher word counts.

READY TO READ MORE
Readers prepare for chapter books with fewer illustrations and longer paragraphs.

This book features sight words from the educator-supported Dolch Sight Words List. This encourages the reader to recognize commonly used vocabulary words, increasing reading speed and fluency.

For more information, please visit passporttoreadingbooks.com.

Enjoy the journey!

Little, Brown and Company

Hachette Book Group
237 Park Avenue, New York, NY 10017
Visit our website at lb-kids.com
mylittlepony.com

Little, Brown and Company is a division of Hachette Book Group, Inc.
The Little, Brown name and logo are trademarks of Hachette Book Group, Inc.

The publisher is not responsible for websites (or their content)
that are not owned by the publisher.

First Edition: April 2014

Library of Congress Control Number: 2013027772

ISBN 978-0-316-36885-8

10 9 8 7 6 5 4 3

CW

Printed in the United States of America

Passport to Reading titles are leveled by independent reviewers applying the standards developed by Irene Fountas and Gay Su Pinnell in *Matching Books to Readers: Using Leveled Books in Guided Reading*, Heinemann, 1999.

Licensed By:

PONIES LOVE PETS!

by Emily C. Hughes

LITTLE, BROWN AND COMPANY
New York Boston

Attention, My Little Pony fans!
Look for these items when you read this book.
Can you spot them all?

alligator

cattle

tortoise

phoenix

These ponies are best friends.

They love to laugh together.

They also love to play with their pets!

The ponies and their pets are
always there to help one another.

Angel is Fluttershy's pet bunny.
He can be a little bossy.

But Angel makes Fluttershy
feel better when she is sad.

Pinkie Pie has a pet alligator named Gummy.
Most ponies would not want an alligator
for a pet, but Gummy is special.
He has no teeth!

It is lucky because he LOVES to bite!

Twilight Sparkle has Owlowiscious. He helps her by bringing books from the library.

At first, he and Spike did not get along, but now they are good friends.

A pony like Applejack needs
a good work dog like Winona!
Winona helps the Apple family
herd the cattle.

The Apple family got Winona
when she was a puppy.
She loves to run and leap and
have her belly scratched!

Rainbow Dash wants a pet as fast and cool as she is, like a falcon or a bat.

She has a contest to find the best animal.
Fluttershy has lots of ideas.

Soon Rainbow Dash meets Tank,
a tortoise who saves her
when a rock falls on her wing.

Tank may be slow,

but Rainbow Dash fixes that.

She turns him into a flying tortoise!

Opalescence is Rarity's cat.
She helps make beautiful
dresses for the other ponies.

The cat does not like to get wet.

She also does not like to do chores.

But there is nothing she hates
more than when someone tries
to steal her toys!

It is not just the ponies of Ponyville
who have pets.
Princess Celestia has a phoenix
named Philomena.
Philomena has a special talent.

She can burst into flames!

Philomena sometimes uses that talent to play tricks on the ponies. Fluttershy has never seen anything like it!

Even Spike has a pet.

Peewee is a baby phoenix.

Spike rescued Peewee back
when he was still an egg.

Pets are hard work!

But the ponies love them.

And the pets love the ponies!

Because friendship is magic, and
pets are a very special kind of friend!